*In memory of Dr. Thomas C. Tacha and to all those who give of their time and energy
to help wild creatures survive in their remaining natural habitat.* — S.L.

For John — S.G.

Special thanks to Dona Lakin Tracy, whose dedication to birds of prey was the
inspiration for this book. — Suzie Gilbert

I owe thanks to Suzie Gilbert and Gigi Giacomara for sharing their expertise and many wonderful
photographs of raptors; to Jeani Garrett and Dickie Neville, who were patient while I photographed
them for reference images to create the main characters in the story; to Jean Marie Hing at
Liberty Wildlife Rehabilitation Foundation, who allowed me to photograph some of the raptors housed
there, and who reviewed my illustrations on several occasions in an effort to keep them accurate;
to Sandy Cate and other volunteers at Adobe Mountain Wildlife Center; to Dan LaGrange and
Ray (his red-tailed hawk); to Mrs. Robert Moore and the Wingfields, both of Virginia, who allowed me
to tramp around their farms to take photos of barns and country landscapes; to Susan Hall,
an elementary school librarian for her help and advise; and last, but most importantly, to Victoria Rock,
who recognized this wonderful manuscript as one that I would love to illustrate. — Sylvia Long

Book design by Jennifer West and Lael Robertson
Typeset in Journal and Stempel Schneidler
Printed in Hong Kong
The illustrations in this book were rendered
in pen and ink and watercolor.

Library of Congress Cataloging-in-Publication Data
Gilbert, Suzie.
    Hawk hill / by Suzie Gilbert; illustrated by Sylvia Long.
    p.   cm.
    Summary: Pete moves to a new town and discovers a rehabilitation center for birds of prey.
    ISBN: 0-8118-0839-4
    [1. Hawks–Fiction. 2. Friendship–Fiction. 3. Moving, Household–Fiction.]
    I. Long, Sylvia, ill. II. Title.
    PZ7.G377Haw   1996
    [Fic]–dc20   96-5214
    CIP   AC

Distributed in Canada by Raincoast Books
8680 Cambie Street, Vancouver B.C. V6P 6M9

Distributed in Australia and New Zealand
by CIS Cardigan Street
245-249 Cardigan Street, Carlton 3053 Australia

10 9 8 7 6 5 4 3 2 1

Chronicle Books
275 Fifth Street, San Francisco, CA 94103

Hawk Hill

by Suzie Gilbert

illustrated by Sylvia Long

CHRONICLE BOOKS · SAN FRANCISCO

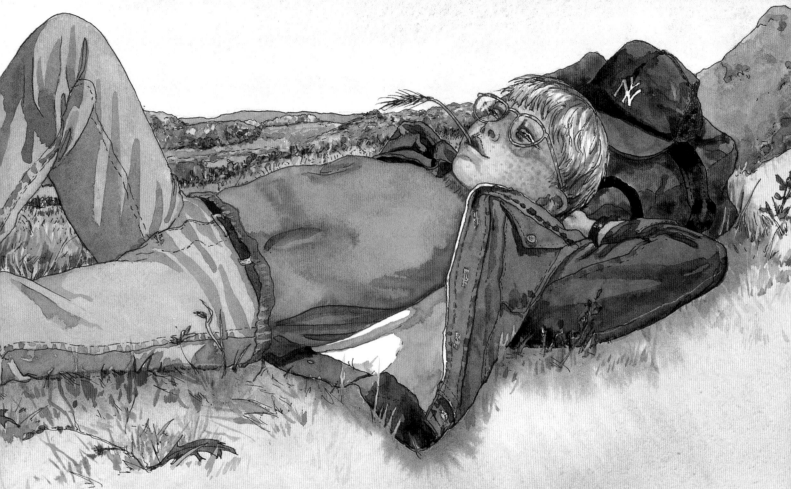

Pete's family moved to a new town just as the leaves on the trees started changing colors. His parents told him that soon he would make lots of friends, but Pete wasn't so sure. Whenever anyone tried to talk to him Pete would just smile and look at the floor. After they had gone away he would think of what he could have said, but by that time it was too late.

Every day after school Pete climbed to the top of a hill near his new house and watched for hawks, just like he used to do with his best friend Jack Maloney. He would lie back, put a long stem of grass between his teeth, and wait. He never tired of watching them glide gracefully through the sky.

One day Pete decided to take a new road home. As he was walking by
an old farmhouse he thought he heard the cry of a hawk. Pete followed
the sound and crept quietly around the house until he came to an overgrown
back lawn. What he saw there made his mouth drop open.

There was not one hawk but three, all tied to their perches by soft
leather leg straps. The hawks stared fiercely at Pete, as if daring him to come
closer. Pete didn't move. He thought if he went any closer he'd either
scare them or, more likely, make them mad, so he stayed where he was and
just looked. The hawks stayed where they were and just looked back.

After a while Pete decided to sit down and make himself more comfortable. The hawks didn't seem to mind, so he lay back, stuck a long stem of grass between his teeth, and watched as they rustled their feathers and stared at the sky.

Suddenly Pete heard a commotion coming from the front of the house. He heard squealing brakes, a slamming door, then voices and footsteps. The voices and footsteps got louder.

Before Pete had time to move a woman was hurrying toward him, followed by a man carrying something wrapped in a blue blanket. The woman saw Pete and gave him a look as fierce as a hawk. "Don't touch the birds!" she snapped. She and the man hurried past Pete and disappeared into the barn. Pete wondered what they had in the blanket.

The barn was cool and quiet and empty. At least, Pete thought it
was empty. He looked into the first stall, expecting to see a horse, and found
nothing. But Pete, who was used to looking up at the sky, looked up at the
ceiling. There, watching him from a wooden beam, was a vulture.

Pete had never seen a vulture up close but his bird books were full
of pictures of them. He recognized the glossy black feathers, the bright red
head and neck, and the powerful beak. Pete couldn't believe his luck.
He looked into the next stall and there, watching him from a wooden beam,
were two owls.

Pete walked down the barn aisle, looking into every stall. Each one
held a hawk, an owl, or a vulture, sometimes two or three. As Pete neared
the end of the barn he heard voices. He followed them until he came
to an open door.

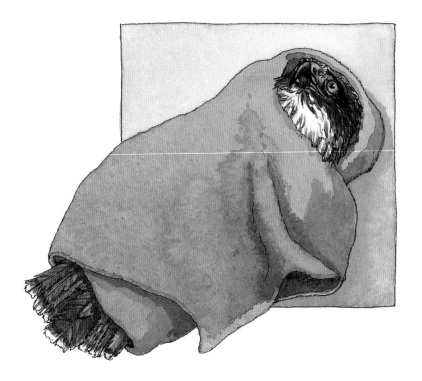

Inside the door was a hospital room, with bright white cabinets and the faint smell of medicine. The man and woman were bent over a gleaming silver table. On the table was the blue blanket, and in the blue blanket was a very large hawk.

The hawk was hurt. It barely moved as the man held it and the woman removed a bullet from its broken wing. Only once did the woman look up. As she was reaching for a bandage she suddenly stopped and looked right at Pete, who was watching silently from the doorway. Pete held his breath, afraid she would order him out of the barn, but she only stared at him briefly before returning to her work.

Finally she was finished. Pete watched her pick the hawk up, put it gently into a cage, and shut the door. By the time she turned around, Pete was gone.

The next day after school Pete hurried back to the barn. He had thought about the hawk with the broken wing so much that by the time he reached the hospital room he was breathless with worry. When he looked into the cage Pete let out a sigh of relief. The hawk let out an angry screech.

Pete pulled his bird book out of his backpack and spent the next hour wandering through the barn, looking up the names of the birds he couldn't identify. Barred Owl. Sharp-shinned Hawk. American Kestrel. Osprey.

He was so absorbed that he didn't see the woman until she was nearly beside him. She paused for an instant, looked down at his bird book, then continued past him without a word. Pete wanted to talk to her but he couldn't think of the right thing to say, so he just watched her as she disappeared into the hospital room. After a moment, he put his book away and walked home.

From then on Pete arrived at the barn every afternoon at precisely 3:25. He would hurry past the farmhouse, leave his backpack at the barn door and head straight for the hospital room to check on the hawk with the broken wing. He had named her Maloney, after his best friend Jack Maloney, and he liked to think that every day she screeched a little less loudly at him. There were other injured birds in the hospital room — owls, a vulture, even an eagle — but he felt a special bond with Maloney.

Pete and the woman never spoke, even though he saw her each day and often felt her watching him as he watched the birds. One day Pete waited until she went into the hospital room. He took a few minutes to get his courage together, then followed her in. She was standing by the table holding an owl with a bandaged leg. She looked up. Pete hoped that she would say something first, but she just stared at him with her fierce eyes and said nothing.

Pete didn't know how to begin. There were so many things he wanted to tell her. He wanted to tell her that he didn't mind his new house so much anymore because it was only a ten minute walk from her barn. That he couldn't wait for the end of the school day because now he had somewhere to go. That just walking into the hospital room and seeing Maloney took away his loneliness. He took a deep breath, ready to tell her all of this, but it didn't come out that way.

"Hi," said Pete.

"Hi," said the woman.

As Pete stood awkwardly, wondering what to do next, the woman glanced up at him again. "I could use some help here," she said.

Pete thought she must be talking to someone behind him so he turned around, but there was no one there.

"Me? " he asked.

"I don't see anyone else," she answered.

The woman wrapped the owl in a blanket so it couldn't move. "If you'll keep him still I'll change the bandage on his leg," she said. As Pete steadied the owl it swiveled its head around and stared into his eyes. Pete thought he'd never seen anything so wild and beautiful.

"What's his name?" Pete whispered.

"He's not mine to name," said the woman. "He's a wild bird. When his leg has healed I'll let him go." When she was done, the woman took the owl from Pete and put it back in a cage.

"Was I okay?" asked Pete anxiously. "Did I do it right?"

"You did very well," said the woman.

"Would you like me to hold another one?" he asked.

"Not today," she replied.

"What about tomorrow?" said Pete. "Could I help you again?"

"If you'd like," said the woman.

The woman's name was Mary, and she knew almost everything there was to know about birds. Every day she taught Pete more about raptors, the birds of prey that hunt for their food. He learned how to feed them, how to care for them, how to hold them when they didn't want to be held.

"They're not pets," said Mary. "They don't like to be touched. They're wild creatures and we should appreciate them for what they are."

Pete was surprised at how often strangers hurried into the barn with an injured bird wrapped in a towel or a jacket. There were kestrels that had been hit by cars, owls that had eaten poisoned rats, an eagle that had been shot.

"Why would someone shoot an eagle?" asked Pete.

"I don't know," answered Mary.

One day, as Pete reached for a bowl in Maloney's cage, she lashed out and cut his finger. Silently Pete went to the sink and washed the blood away, then wrapped his finger neatly with gauze and tape. He opened the cage door again and, making sure he moved more slowly, removed the bowl and closed the door. He turned to find Mary watching him.

"It was my fault," said Pete. "I moved too fast."

"But not the second time," said Mary.

"I think Maloney's much better," said Pete.

"Remember," said Mary gently. "She's a wild bird. She can't stay."

"I know," said Pete.

When Pete wasn't helping Mary with the other birds he sat in the
hospital near Maloney. Pete thought he and Maloney had a lot in common,
since they'd both arrived at Mary's on the same day and had both moved
into a new home without really wanting to. Pete continued to offer his
friendship to Maloney, even though Maloney didn't seem to want to take it.

Pete no longer worried about saying the right thing to Mary, and
no longer felt he had to search for words to fill a silence. "Sometimes I have
trouble talking to people," he admitted. "I don't know what to say."

"Then don't say anything," said Mary. "Most people talk too much."

After the first snow, Mary removed Maloney's bandage and put her in a
stall in the barn.

"When will you let her go?" asked Pete.

"In the spring," said Mary. "It will be easier for her to find food then."
Pete sighed with relief. Spring was a long time away.

Each day, Pete arrived at the barn to find Maloney standing by the
small window at the back of her stall. He would lean against the door and
watch as she stared at the old road that led through the woods, hoping she
would turn and stare at him instead.

"What's she looking for?" he asked.

"I'll show you," said Mary.

Mary and Pete left the barn and climbed to the top of a nearby hill. "I used to come here after school," said Pete. "Before I met you."

"This is Hawk Hill," said Mary. "When the birds have recovered this is where I let them go."

Pete looked up at the sky and saw a hawk circling above them, its wings tinted orange by the setting sun. "That's a Rough-legged Hawk," said Mary. "Do you know how you can tell?" That afternoon Pete learned how to identify birds of prey as they flew above him, and he and Mary stood on the hill and practiced until it was too dark to see.

That winter a cold north wind brought snow and sleet as the wild birds huddled together in Mary's barn. Maloney stayed by her window, watching as the sun grew pale and the trees sparkled with ice. Occasionally she would turn and stare at Pete, hovering outside the door in heavy boots and an old coat, and Pete would grin with happiness and continue his chores.

Sometimes in the late afternoon when the air grew bitter, Mary and Pete carried armloads of wood up the stairs to the farmhouse. While Mary made hot chocolate Pete pushed the logs into the old woodstove until the fire was blazing and his face stung with the heat. As they sat deep in the soft cushions of her old chairs Mary told stories. How the Iroquois believed the sun was carried on the wings of an eagle. How the Sioux believed an owl guarded the gate to the Milky Way. How once there was a land where wild birds were so numerous they darkened the sky and made the wind blow with their wings.

Spring came early that year, and one day Pete found Mary waiting for him holding Maloney in her arms. Attached to Maloney's legs were a pair of thin leather straps and a long line.

"She needs some exercise," said Mary.

When they got to the field below Hawk Hill, Mary took Maloney from Pete and handed him the line. "When I let her go," said Mary, "let the line uncoil and make sure it doesn't get tangled. Are you ready?"

Pete nodded and with one smooth motion Mary threw Maloney into the air. As Maloney spread her wings and flew away from them Pete felt a hot prickle of fear, but moments later she slowed and landed on the grass. Pete felt a rush of relief: he hadn't lost her after all.

For the next month, Mary and Pete exercised the birds that had healed well enough to start flying. Pete learned how to catch them in their cages, how to fasten their leg straps, and how to throw them high into the air to give them a longer flight. He watched as Maloney grew stronger and more graceful, and before long he could see no trace of her broken wing.

Finally, one afternoon, Maloney came to the end of the line and stayed briefly in the air, straining to break free. Pete looked at Mary, knowing what she was going to say.

"I think she's ready," said Mary. "We'll let her go tomorrow."

The next day Pete was silent as he carried Maloney to the top of Hawk Hill. He hardly noticed when Mary pointed to the perfect blue sky and the fields covered with wildflowers.

"It's best for her," said Mary.

"I know," said Pete, trying to believe that when he opened his arms Maloney would stay with him. Pete looked down into her fierce, unblinking eyes, and with one smooth motion threw her into the air. Maloney stretched her wings, soared upward, and flew away. For long minutes Pete scanned the sky, waiting for her to circle around and return to him. Finally he looked up at Mary.

"She didn't even look back," said Pete.

"She's going home," said Mary.

Pete didn't show up at the barn the next afternoon, or the one after that, so on the third day Mary went looking for him. She found him sitting alone on Hawk Hill, watching the sky.

"I thought maybe she'd come back," said Pete. "Not to stay. Just to let me know she's okay."

"She might be far away by now," said Mary.

"Maybe not," said Pete.

"I could use some help with the other birds," said Mary.

Pete shook his head. "Maybe tomorrow," he said. "I think I'll just stay here for today."

For the rest of the week Pete climbed to the top of the hill and waited, but Maloney didn't return.

Mary did. Late one afternoon she appeared again, cradling something in her shirt. She sat down next to Pete and held out her hands.

Nestled inside them was a tiny hawk. "Someone found her by the side of the road," said Mary. "I thought we could call her Little Maloney."

The orphan looked up at Pete with a fierce and fearless gaze. "We can't," said Pete. "She's not ours to name."

"She can be ours," said Mary, "just for a little while."

Pete walked down the hill with Mary, carefully holding Little Maloney close to his chest. "When did she get here?" asked Pete. "Have you fed her yet?"

"Not yet," said Mary. "I was waiting for you."

Raptors are among the finest athletes in the bird kingdom. They soar and swoop, bank and turn, climb into and drop out of the sky, all at breathtaking speed. Those lucky enough to have seen such a sight might find it hard to imagine the same bird lying on the ground, injured and unable to fly. Yet it happens all too often, as birds of every kind continue to collide with our modern world. Those who care for injured wildlife are called rehabilitators, and they face a difficult task. It takes knowledge, skill, and patience. It takes dedication, for wild animals have no owners, and rehabilitators must pay for food and medicine out of their own pockets or by asking the public for donations. Not all raptors survive their injuries, and not all can return to the wild. But those who care for them know that with enough help, hope and luck, many injured birds will fly again.

RED-TAILED HAWK

The most commonly seen North American hawk, the Red-tailed Hawk is able to survive extremes in temperature, hunt a wide range of prey, and live comfortably near humans. It prefers a mix of open land and forest and eats mostly small mammals and snakes.

ROUGH-LEGGED HAWK

The Rough-legged Hawk is a large Northern species that spends the winters in the United States and the summers in Alaska and Canada. It nests in cliffs and searches for small mammals by hovering above open fields.

BROAD-WINGED HAWK

Broad-winged Hawks are small, quiet forest hawks that hunt frogs, snakes and rodents. In the fall, they gather in groups of thousands and migrate to Central and South America, providing a thrilling sight to those who gather to watch from sites such as the famous Hawk Mountain in Eastern Pennsylvania.

NORTHERN GOSHAWK

Maneuvering through the forest at lightning speed, Northern Goshawks use the surprise attack to capture medium-sized birds and mammals. The fastest and fiercest of the woodland hawks, they are known for defending their territory aggressively from humans.

COOPER'S HAWK

The Cooper's Hawk has the short wings and long tail of a woodland hawk and is expert at ambushing its prey. The eyes of the Cooper's Hawk, like those of the Sharp-shinned Hawk and the Northern Goshawk, are grey at birth, turn bright yellow by the age of one year, darken to orange through maturity and finally turn red at old age.

SHARP-SHINNED HAWK

Small and secretive, the Sharp-shinned Hawk flies quietly through dense woodlands, seeking to capture small birds and avoid capture by larger raptors. Although most female birds of prey are slightly larger than their male counterparts, the female sharp-shin is almost twice as heavy as her mate.

NORTHERN HARRIER

Slender and agile, Northern Harriers have a round, owl-like face.
This facial shape focuses sound and allows them to locate their prey by
hearing. Hunting at dusk along with bats and owls, they fly over wet,
swampy ground looking for frogs, lizards, birds and small mammals.

PEREGRINE FALCON

Found almost all over the world, Peregrine Falcons even nest on the bridges
and skyscrapers of New York City. Hunters of other birds, they circle high
in the sky, then spot and drop down on their prey in dives that can reach
speeds of 200 miles per hour.

AMERICAN KESTREL

North America's smallest raptor is the American Kestrel, a colorful little
falcon that hovers over open fields looking for mice, lizards and grasshoppers.
Unlike most birds of prey, male and female kestrels are colored differently:
the male's wings are bluish-grey while the female's are reddish-brown.

TURKEY VULTURE

Turkey Vultures are scavengers that use their keen sense of smell to locate
carcasses. They nest in logs or caves and begin their days by perching on a
cliff or tree limb, then spreading their wings to catch the morning sun.

OSPREY

Ospreys are large raptors that are found nearly all over the world and
feed only on fish. Plunging into the water from 50 to 100 feet in the air, they
use their long legs, curved talons and feet lined with tiny spines to grasp
their prey and carry it away.

BALD EAGLE

Bald Eagles are born dark and usually do not attain their famous white heads
and tails until their sixth year. Although they are skilled hunters of large fish
and waterbirds, they are not above stealing a meal from Ospreys,
sometimes in mid-air.

GREAT HORNED OWL

One of the largest and most powerful of the North American owls, the Great
Horned Owl flies silently through dark forests in search of birds, mammals,
hawks and smaller owls. It is easily recognized by its size and distinctive ear
tufts, and on a still night its hooting can be heard as far as a mile away.

BARRED OWL

Smaller and gentler than the Great Horned Owl, the brown-eyed Barred Owl
prefers to live near wooded swamps, occasionally hunting on cloudy days
as well as at night, dusk, and dawn. As with all owls, its softly fringed feathers
allow it to fly nearly soundlessly.